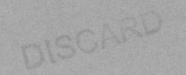

CREAMED TUNA·FISH & PEAS ON·TOAST

Philip Christian Stead

A Neal Porter Book
ROARING BROOK PRESS
New York

Stead

For So and So
& You Know Who

WILD MAN JACK was not easy to please.

He never ate apples, mackerel, or cheese.

But Wild Man Jack
hated one dish the most—

"Creamed tuna fish and peas on toast!"

Susie asked her dad on Sunday,
"Wild Man Jack, what will you do if Mama Jane
cooks creamed tuna fish and peas on toast?"

Wild Man Jack replied,

"I'll scream and complain 'cause I hate it the most!"

Danny asked his dad on Monday,
"Wild Man Jack, what will you do if Mama Jane
cooks creamed tuna fish and peas on toast?"

Wild Man Jack replied,
"I'll steam and I'll wheeze 'cause I hate it the most!"

Nancy asked her dad on Tuesday,
"Wild Man Jack, what will you do if Mama Jane
cooks creamed tuna fish and peas on toast?"

Wild Man Jack replied,
"I'll brandish my spoon 'cause I hate it the most!"

Margie asked her dad on Wednesday,
"Wild Man Jack, what will you do if Mama Jane
cooks creamed tuna fish and peas on toast?"

Wild Man Jack replied,
"I'll dig a deep hole 'cause I hate it the most!"

Bobby asked his dad on Thursday,
"Wild Man Jack, what will you do if Mama Jane
cooks creamed tuna fish and peas on toast?"

Wild Man Jack replied,
"I'll chisel a stone 'cause I hate it the most!"

On Friday, Mama Jane smiled and said,
"Now, Wild Man Jack, don't lose your head.
I've made you the dish that you love the most..."

"Uh-oh!

Uh-oh!

Uh-oh!

Uh-oh!

Uh-oh!"

"Creamed tuna fish and peas on toast!"

Jack screamed,   complained,

steamed,   wheezed,

brandished
his spoon,

dug a deep hole,

and on Saturday morning he paid his respects.

He said a few words, bowed his head,

and buried the dish that he hated the most—

"Creamed tuna fish and peas on toast!"